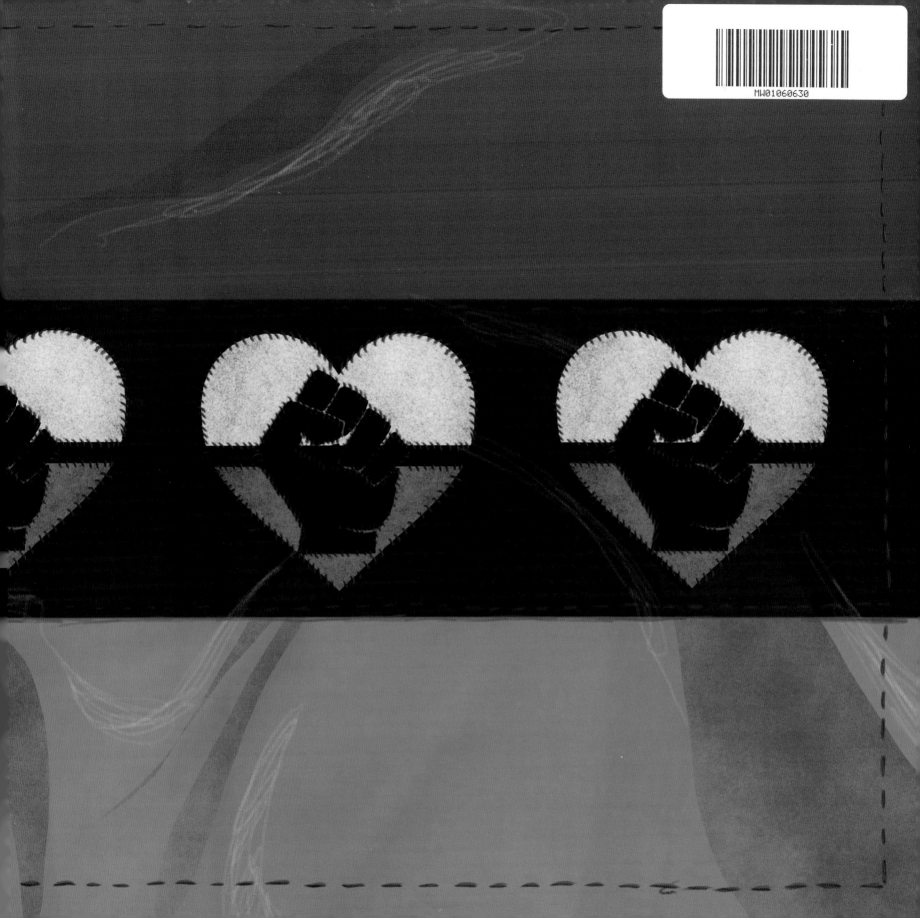

For Larry, my brisket pitmaster. 143. —N. T.

For my partner, baby boy, and family, who I will
forever draw strength and inspiration from. —D. J. O.

Library of Congress Cataloging-in-Publication Data

Names: Tripplett, Natasha, author. | O'Brien, Daniel J., illustrator.
Title: Juneteenth is / by Natasha Tripplett ; illustrated by Daniel J.
  O'Brien.
Description: San Francisco : Chronicle Books, 2024. | Includes
  bibliographical references.
Identifiers: LCCN 2023019720 | ISBN 9781797216805 (hardcover)
  Subjects: LCSH: Juneteenth--Juvenile fiction. | African Americans--
  Anniversaries, etc.--Juvenile fiction. | African American
  families--Juvenile fiction. | CYAC: Juneteenth--Fiction. | African
  Americans--Anniversaries, etc.--Fiction. | African American
  families--Fiction. | LCGFT: Picture books.
Classification: LCC PZ7.1.T7565 Ju 2024 | DDC 813.6
  [Fic]--dc23/eng/20230427
LC record available at https://lccn.loc.gov/2023019720

Manufactured in China.

MIX
Paper | Supporting
responsible forestry
FSC™ C104723
www.fsc.org

Design by Jay Marvel.
Typeset in Athelas.
The illustrations in this book were rendered digitally.

10 9 8 7 6 5 4 3 2

Chronicle books and gifts are available at special quantity discounts to
corporations, professional associations, literacy programs, and other
organizations. For details and discount information, please contact our
premiums department at corporatesales@chroniclebooks.com or at
1-800-759-0190.

Chronicle Books LLC
680 Second Street
San Francisco, California 94107

Chronicle Books—we see things differently.
Become part of our community at www.chroniclekids.com.

Juneteenth Is

Written by Natasha Tripplett
Illustrated by Daniel J. O'Brien

chronicle books · san francisco

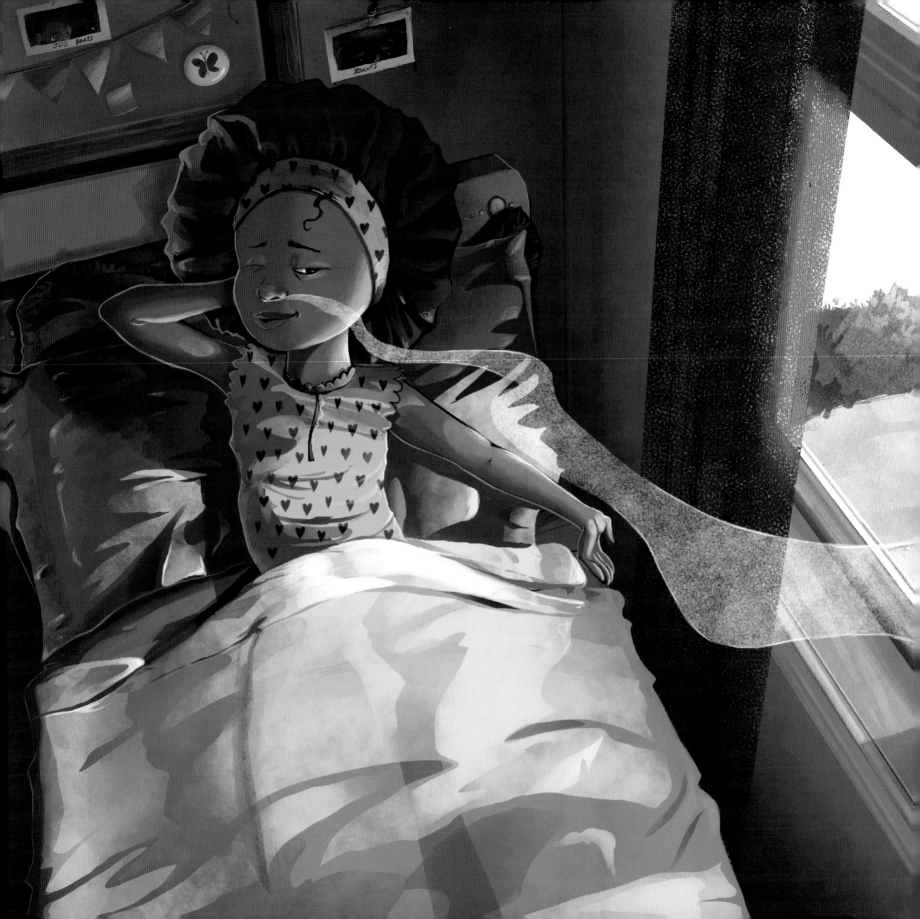

On Juneteenth, I awake to the smoky smell of Daddy's slow-cooking brisket.

Facing the rising sun, peeking over the hills.
Jubilee has begun.

I skip ahead to the music as Daddy carries the chairs.
Juneteenth is the perfect sidewalk spot.

A parade of steppers, dancers,
singers, drummers all march.

Colorful candies rain on the crowd.
Horns belt out a freedom song.

A queen in braids winks as she pop-locks her way past.

Mama calls her a hope for tomorrow.

Black, red, and green flags
welcome us to the cool breeze of
Granddaddy's front porch.

Hugs and fist bumps.
"Girl, you gettin' tall."
Forehead kisses and hugs again.
Warmth floods my soul.
Juneteenth is being thankful
to be together.

Juneteenth is the house getting louder
as more cousins, aunties and uncles,
neighbors and play-cousins arrive.
Stevie gives us "Something to Say" from the boom box,
as the snare beat brings us back in tune.

Juneteenth is the ladies
singing in the kitchen.

Juneteenth is my
favorite uncle's jokes.
Sitting on the curb,
watching the game.
Watermelon so sweet, you
close your eyes to chew.

Granny calls us in to eat.
"Go wash your hands, we 'bout to pray."
Juneteenth is prayer.

Juneteenth is generations of family recipes.
Secret rub on finger-lickin' chicken,
juicy mouth-on-fire hot links, mac 'n' cheese,
collard greens, potato salad, smoky brisket,
barbecue baked beans, honey corn bread,
and stories from the past.

Red in the sauce, red in the soda,
red in the watermelon, red velvet cake.
Red in the suffering.

Juneteenth is the history lesson
not taught at school.

Granddaddy's deep voice
reminds us why we're here.

"It's not the slam of dominoes or
the slam dunk of the mac 'n' cheese—
sho' was good though . . . It's about
the door of opportunity no longer
slamming in our faces."

Juneteenth is remembering lives
long before our memories.
Sweat on our brows, cotton in our fingers,
the straw that broke our mighty back.

A lump creeps into my throat.

The Proclamation took
two years to be proclaimed.

June 19, 1865—the American Day of Freedom.
General Granger rode into Galveston, Texas, and
read the order: Slaves are free.

Juneteenth is freedom shackled to a
Parks, King, and Obama future.

Former slaves marched in
the first Juneteenth parade.

We have been
marching ever since.

We march in celebration.
We march in unity.
Proudly, we march on the
land of the free in bravery.

Juneteenth is all of us.

We are America.

ON THE SIGNIFICANCE OF RED

The color red is prominent at many Juneteenth celebrations as a symbol of the bloodshed, grief, and anguish experienced by enslaved people. Red foods such as barbecue, strawberries, watermelon, and red velvet cake have made their way onto Juneteenth plates. Red drinks such as hibiscus tea, red Kool-Aid, and red sodas often accompany the Juneteenth meal. Many people also wear red clothing to respect the past. Some historians believe the significance of the color red came with the enslaved people across the Atlantic. In many West African cultures, red is a symbol of strength, spirituality, and ancestral connectedness.

It is imperative to remember that Juneteenth is so much more than just the food we eat. Celebrating Juneteenth is a privilege that honors the legacy of the people who made this holiday special. It is about family, love, and community. We gather together on Juneteenth to share a history that unifies us all.

SELECTED BIBLIOGRAPHY

Barrett, Claire. "Why You Celebrate Juneteenth with a Red Drink." HistoryNet. June 15, 2022.

Edmonds, Lauren. "A Food Historian Explains Why the Color Red Plays an Important Role during Juneteenth Celebrations." Business Insider India. June 19, 2022.

Necole, Shaunda. "13 Juneteenth Red Foods and Drinks and Watermelon Red Soda." The Soul Food Pot. Updated June 12, 2023.

Taylor, Nicole. "Hot Links and Red Drinks: The Rich Food Tradition of Juneteenth." *The New York Times*. June 13, 2017.

Whaley, Natelegé. "The History behind Staple Juneteenth Foods: BBQ, Watermelon and Red Drinks." Black Restaurant Week. Accessed October 18, 2022.